Pushing The Boundaries

Leigh Temple

Published by Leigh Temple, 2023.

PUSHING THE BOUNDARIES

First edition. June 8, 2023.

Copyright © 2023 Leigh Temple.

ISBN: 979-8223949596

Written by Leigh Temple.

Also by Leigh Temple

First Time Hotwife In Cancun
Housewife to Hotwife
Becoming a Hotwife - A Wife Transforms Before Her Cuckold Husband's Eyes
Anniversary Swinging: A Couple Look For New Ways To Celebrate
The Cuckold Clinic
Vacation Cuckold
A White Wife Can't Resist
First Time Entered
Cuckold Cleanup
Control
Hotwife Surprise
A Shared Submission
Pushing The Boundaries

Chapter 1

I'm going to tell you about a situation that took place a couple of years ago. It's a story that involves me and my then-fiancée Jemma. It's a time in my life I never want to forget. I'm doing my best to write this to the best of my recollection, and I'm including Jemma's thoughts and feelings, too, as she has been willing to share them with me.

I'll be entirely frank; Jemma is drop-dead gorgeous and a picture of total grace. There's something special about the way it feels just being around her. It's an odd feeling; it can be equal parts intimidating and welcoming all at the same time. Probably the thing about her that stands out most is her exquisite, captivating emerald eyes that compliment her picture-perfect smile. Beyond that, everything is sort of normal, in an extremely hot sort of way. She's naturally a very sporty girl and has a body that would stand out in any outfit. She's a 5'6" brunette, and to say she is a regular gym going is an understatement. Six days a week, every week, she is in the gym. And the girl can seriously squat and deadlift. In fact, that is the reason she has an ass that gets most guys to do a double-take. But the best thing about her, beyond the beautiful eyes and the ass that is actually jaw-dropping, is the fact that although Jemma knows she's attractive, she's actually a really shy and modest girl who never makes a big deal out of her natural beauty, which makes me even prouder to be her fiancé.

We met completely innocently; a random series of events led to us meeting. My manager had moaned for months about wanting to spruce up the office, going on about getting some murals like a lot of other contemporary offices had done. Eventually, he stopped moaning and actually did it. Our company ended up hiring an up-and-coming art studio to do the job. As I walked through the corridors one day at work, I saw her talking to a coworker. Well, I say I saw her. I saw the back of her, which meant I saw that ass. Her big, round, incredibly firm beautiful ass.

The ass that you think can't be that big and that firm at the same time. The ass that does those squats. Anyone, it's fair to say it was the first time her ass got me. When the girl with the ass turned around suddenly and happened to look at me, it was like time slowed down, and I actually spilled some of my coffee. I know it sounds like some really cheesy movie scene, but I genuinely couldn't help it. I saw the ass and was expecting something so different, and then she turned. And there she was, just a very natural, very pretty, clearly shy girl with an insanely hot body. As she looked at me, her gaze felt like a laser burning through me, although that might have been the boiling hot coffee. And true to her kind nature, before I knew it, she had rushed over to make sure I was alright and introduced herself.

The rest was history.

We got talking, and we hit it off. We went on a couple of dates afterward, and when the studio had completed the job, and we had a load of artwork modernizing the walls of our office, Jemma continued to stop by during lunch so we could spend some time together. It was great, especially because I wasn't the brashest guy around, so it was always a bit tough for me. I'd hesitate before asking her out or initiating any type of communication.

We didn't have sex until much later in our story, and it was only then that I found out that she was actually pretty inexperienced in that department. Well, I say pretty inexperienced; she had only been with two guys before she met me. It took me a while to accept or believe that. Not because I doubted her but because we were both close to 30, and you normally don't make it to the end of college without messing around more than a few times. But what really made it hard for me to understand was the fact that Jemma is an absolute stunner. She would have had guys queuing up any day of the week.

Anyway, as I'm sure you can guess from the beautiful ass, the sporty body, the squats, and everything, the sex was amazing and well worth the wait. It's hard to describe it because it won't come out right. But

Jemma really didn't have many fancy moves. She only knew the absolute basics, but the combination of her amazing body and her passion was mind-blowing. I normally have pretty good self-control, but she pushed me to my limits. Once, early on, she looked so damn sexy underneath me that I came in about 20 seconds. I actually lied to her and said I wanted to go down on her some more, which she absolutely loves, by the way, and did that for a good 20 minutes while I recovered from cumming so prematurely. Then I fucked her again and managed to last a slightly more respectable amount of time. I told her the condom had fallen off while I was eating her out, and she never worked it out. To this day, she doesn't know I blew my load in 20 seconds because her body is that fucking hot!

As I said, Jemma was pretty inexperienced but very willing nonetheless. She matched whatever request I had of her in bed and would always put 100% into anything, even new things she had never tried. We kept things relatively tame for quite a long time, mainly because neither of us had a lot of experience, and despite her enthusiasm for anything I suggested, Jemma was never one to make suggestions herself. She was a creative type, but not in that way! I guess, like most couples, we eventually stopped having sex as much. It went from every hour of every day to a few hours every now and again. But it was still something I looked forward to whenever we were together. I've never seen anything quite as mesmerizing as watching her big toned ass slide up and down my cock again and again. She can squat facing away from me and literally bounce her big ass up and down as her tight little pussy slides up and down my shaft. God, it's hot. The hottest thing I've ever seen, in real life on in a fantasy. I've caught myself plenty of times just daydreaming about her body, thinking about all the positions I'd like to see it in or things I'd like to do to it. Eventually, sex would get a little bit stale, if I'm honest. We would just kind of default to missionary and reverse cowgirl during our time together. But even with that, it was still the case that no one I had been with in my past has ever come even close to sex with Jemma.

This, along with the fact that every time I'm with her, it just feels so right, meant that about a year into our relationship, there really was no choice for me but to get down on one knee and propose to her. This made Jemma my fiancée and made me a very lucky man.

So now that you know a little of the backstory, we can move forward to that one fateful day and learn how I discovered my hidden fetish that would dramatically change our relationship forever.

I remember waking up a little groggy that day.

When I stretched over and glanced at my phone on the bedside table, I realized it was getting close to lunchtime, and I remembered that Jemma had taken the car. She said she wanted to drop off a few things at her studio in the morning, then she was going to come back to get me, and we were going for a late lunch with some of our mutual friends.

However, like most days I woke up, I was rock hard down there. I figured I had a good half hour until Jemma was home, maybe longer, so I decided to get to work on my problem. I loaded up my phone's web browser, making sure to go incognito, obviously. I'm not usually a phone porn kind of guy, but I really couldn't be bothered getting up and grabbing my laptop. I guess it's something that's truly remarkable about porn nowadays, you can access it everywhere, on anything, at any time! Not that you always want to, but it's still mind-boggling and super convenient that it is always there and available.

Technology.

So ten minutes or so of watching some pretty bad stuff, and I was just finishing off when I saw a message pop up on the screen from Jemma. She said she was about 5 minutes away. No problem, I thought. I put on something decent and head down to the front door. The lunch wasn't planned as anything special, just a quick hangout with friends, so I didn't need to wear anything special.

When her next message came through, I headed out to be greeted by her lovely smiling face from inside the car. She hopped out, and I hopped into the driver's seat. Jemma was never a fan of driving, and it didn't bother me. But it also gave me a great chance to stop and take note of her sexy sway as she walked around the car; that ass swaying like that is never going to get old.

On the journey, we chatted a little bit about what to expect. We were meeting a group that was a combination of both of our friends. Emma and Braun have been my friends since the start of high school. They got together and ended up getting married after graduation. By that point, I had already introduced them to Jemma, and they both absolutely loved her. We assumed there were going to be lots of discussions about our upcoming wedding, which was starting to approach pretty fast now. Jemma's best friend since elementary school, Tasha, would also be there. We always had to prepare ourselves when Tasha would be around. We're both pretty chilled people, and Tasha was a real bag of energy kind of girl, so we had to prepare to make sure we could match her energy levels.

As we drove along discussing what to expect at lunch, I realized we'd been listening to a sports commentary on the radio for a game that neither of us had any interest in at all.

"Hey babe," I asked, raising an eyebrow. "What station is this?"

"I'm not sure. I just thought you might want to listen to one of those basketball shows in the background."

"Oh, well, that's really sweet!" I genuinely did think this was incredibly thoughtful of her, but I knew for sure that she absolutely hated listening to sports radio. She didn't mind sports, but listening to radio hosts talk about the game the night before and analyzing every event was something she just couldn't get into. "Why don't you change it to your music. Put on a playlist, and let's listen to something fun instead?"

As soon as I said that, I was immediately rewarded with a nice peck on the cheek. I was the man. Sometimes with Jemma, it honestly felt like I couldn't do a thing wrong.

Except, I wasn't perfect. In fact, I was far from it.

As I drove off the highway exit and down the ramp, I knew we were five minutes from the restaurant; I heard the sports talk show station stop suddenly, clearly when Jemma changed the car's audio input. I should have known what was about to happen as she selected the option for "Bluetooth."

The car stereo immediately searched for and connected to the phone. My phone.

Apparently, the car's Bluetooth always connects to the phone it was last connected to first, so in this case, mine. If you want to connect a different one, you have to manually switch the phone it connects to, something that you can only do after the fact. Another fact I discovered that day was that if you had a video playing on your phone but you just turned it off, it's no problem at all for your helpful car. As soon as the Bluetooth connects, it will resume playing for you right from the moment where you left off.

All I heard as I was driving along was the abrupt and breathy moaning I recognized from about an hour before, followed by, "Yes, fill me up, baby!"

Then an equally breathy male voice said, "Are you really sure this is what you want?"

"Yeah... and it's what my husband wants too!"

I was so shocked at that point I actually swerved the car. A loud horn blast from the car beside us brought me back to reality, and I steered back to safety and away from danger. I briefly managed to turn my head and look at my fiancée's astonished face. A second later, the conversation coming through the speakers devolved back into loud, incoherent moaning. This went on for about 30 seconds before it reached a crescendo with the male porn star's impressive roar as he, and I can only assume as we just had sound, no video, filled the moaning woman up.

Once I had managed to steady the car, we both just sat in silence. I was pretty shocked Jemma didn't say anything. I eventually remembered there was a mute button on the steering wheel; if only I'd done that a few seconds earlier, life might have been very different. I did look, but I just assumed Jemma still had the shocked look on her face the entire way to the restaurant.

As I pulled into the parking lot, Jemma still hadn't said anything. I eventually plucked up the courage to finally turn my head to look at her. As I looked, all I saw was her just staring stone-faced at the dashboard.

I followed her eyes and realized the video's title was displayed on the screen. It was there in crystal clear HD quality font. Now it was in plain sight for my poor innocent fiancée to see. "Cuckold husband shares wife for the first time." I hit the ignition and turned the engine off as I took a deep breath and tried to hide my fear, but as soon as I pushed the fear down, the embarrassment swept over me.

It felt like a million thoughts were running through my head at that moment. The most terrifying of them was the awful thought of Jemma breaking up with me now because she'd seen the sort of porn I watch. She had learned my kinkiest fantasy by chance, and I was completely unprepared for her to find out. All I could think was, is she going to break up with me because she now knows I clearly watch porn when she's not around? Was our wedding still on? Why the fuck did I not close the incognito browser when I had finished? And why the fuck does my car's Bluetooth not prompt you to ask which phone it should connect to?

These questions flashed through my head like a dingy motel's flickering light bulb, flickering far too fast for me to come up with any form of rational answer.

I remember, at some point, I just gave up, leaned forward, and put my head in my hands. I was equal parts mortified, embarrassed, and lost for words. I had been completely done by the same technology I had been praising when I woke up. Remember when I said how impressed I was with the fact modern technology means "You can access porn anywhere!" Ugh. What a dumbass!

It was Jemma who finally broke the awkward silence. As her signature calming voice broke through my self-loathing, I glanced over at her.

"So, what's a cuckold?"

I blinked at her as I did a double take. She didn't seem angry at all. In fact, it looked like she might be trying to hide the tiniest hint of a smile. Maybe life wasn't truly ruined?

"And why is he sharing his wife!?" As she asked the second question, Jemma broke out into uncontrollable laughter. As soon as she did, I couldn't help it; I joined her. Although she was probably laughing at my embarrassment, I was laughing in pure relief.

Jemma had reacted in the best way imaginable, and I couldn't believe how lucky I was.

"So, do you really want to know?" I asked, lifting my head slightly.

"Well, I expect you to tell me... But do it later. I'm not sure it's going to be a suitable conversation for lunch." As she said this, she opened the car door and gracefully exited as I clumsily followed suit, stepping out of my side. "Right now, we're here to meet our friends and have a nice lunch. Absolutely no wife sharing!"

She turned and waved toward our friends, who we could see through the restaurant window, and they waved back. It looked like we would be having this discussion later, so at least I had some time to prepare. I reached for her hand and felt her reaching for mine as we both hurried inside.

Before we managed to get through the door, she gave me another kiss on the cheek and whispered into my ear, "You know I watch some porn when you're not around, too."

I nearly tripped right over the air. I was that surprised at what she had just said. My sweet, innocent fiancee Jemma watched porn? What the actual fuck?!

Chapter 2

Once we got back home, I walked into the living room, took a deep breath, and readied myself on the sofa. I had a feeling this would be one of the most awkward talks we'd ever had. Everything had always just seemed to click with Jemma and me. Everything we'd ever talked about just seemed to fall into place, but her apparent confusion regarding what a "cuckold" even was told me I had some ground to cover with her. She didn't come into the living room immediately; she took a few minutes in the kitchen pouring us some water before she came and sat down next to me, an adorable look of curiosity plastered all over her face.

"So, mister. Spill it!" She said with a hint of a smile as she handed me my glass of water.

"Okay, okay," I said, taking a sip to calm my nerves. "So I might have watched some porn before you got home."

"Come on, baby. I know you watch porn. You're a guy. Did you really think I didn't know you jerk off to porn? Honestly, but you know what I'm really asking!" She said, shooting me a slightly annoyed glare, making it clear the time for avoiding the issue was over.

I gave an awkward smile as I placed my glass of water down on the table. "Alright, well, a cuckold is ... well, it's usually a guy who......urm......."

I was really starting to struggle at this point. It dawned on me that I had never really needed to explain the term to anyone else before. "So it's a guy who likes watching his wife do... urm..... sexual stuff with someone else."

Her eyebrows shot up as fast as lightning.

"Wow. Honestly? Are you sure it's a real thing? It isn't like some sort of fake category?"

"What do you fake category?"

She also put her glass down at this point and paused for a second before responding. "I mean, I don't get it. Surely the most pleasurable thing possible is being the one having sex. Especially with your partner!

Right? It's pretty obvious that there can't be any way it's more pleasurable watching someone else have sex with your wife. I don't get it; how can they even compare?"

I squirmed uncomfortably in my seat. I was trying my best to remain calm and look her in the eye while admitting to, without a doubt, one of the weirdest fetishes I had. "Well... urm... I actually find the idea hot. And I think quite a lot of guys do, too, if I'm honest. I mean, that's why there's an entire category of porn dedicated to it, right? And there's a lot of cuckold porn; it's a huge category! Then there are the bits that are linked to it. You can even lookup hotwife—"

I had to stop myself from speaking at this point. I didn't know how much Jemma wanted to know or how much I should be telling her about this in the first place.

"Hotwife?" She said as she tilted her head to the side as she heard the word. "Oh, so that would be what we call the wife of a cuckold in this sort of situation?"

I nodded before closing my eyes and letting a deep sigh out. "You got it! Anyway, now that we're done with that—"

With that, I stood up, my signal that the end of the conversation had arrived, well, at least it had arrived for me. Jemma clearly had other ideas as she pushed me gently with her hands, signaling to me that this was not, in fact, going to be the end of the conversation.

She paused momentarily before looking me straight in the eyes and asked, "So, are you a cuckold?"

"What the fuck?" I probably looked as surprised as I was. I mean, I was unbelievably surprised at what Jemma had just asked. I wasn't shocked by the question, in the sense that I watched a lot of cuckold porn, so I guess I needed to ask myself that question. What truly shocked me was hearing those words coming out of my innocent fiancee's mouth. "No. Urm.. No. I think I just like watching that type of porn."

"Okay, let me rephrase that," Jemma replied. "Would you like to see me with another guy?" She was somehow asking that question with a perfectly stone face.

At that point, I simply couldn't find the right words. I was just sitting on the sofa, staring up at the most beautiful woman I've ever been with as her eyes pierced straight into mine as she tried to get me to spill the beans on what I knew was my most perverted fetish. I just sat on the sofa, unable to speak. That was twice today. I'd been genuinely speechless.

Jemma leaned forward at this point.

"Babe, you do, don't you?" She paused to brush away a lock of soft hair from her face as she leaned in even closer. "Even if you don't want to be honest with me, this little guy down here seems to be feeling pretty honest."

I looked down just in time to see her place a finger on the tip of my cock, which was threatening to burst through my jeans. She just smiled as she added, "As usual."

I sort of shrunk back into the sofa a little. I genuinely hadn't noticed I was getting turned on by her line of questioning. I also couldn't work out if she was just making fun of me or if this was something else altogether. I was honestly so confused by the whole situation that I had no idea what to think. Jemma had never done anything like this before. Stood in front of me now was a different woman; she wasn't the same timid fiancée I had proposed to.

Slowly I felt her hand start to unbutton my pants and slide them down my legs. Almost instantly, she was pulling at my boxers. As soon as she pulled them down over the tip of my cock it sprung up in front of her face, rock hard and swollen. I was now staring down at one of the hottest sights I had ever seen as my fiancée reflexively bit her lip in response to seeing my swollen cock.

Before I could say a word, she leaned in and slid her tongue out, giving the tip of my cock a playful lick. The feeling of her tongue on the head of my cock sent shivers up my spine. It was unbelievable. Normally it would excite me, but it was on another level right now. I couldn't help but think to myself shouldn't she be angry? Or even disgusted at what I'd just told her? Shouldn't she hate me for what I thought?"

"So baby, do you want to watch me lick another cock then? Just. Like—" Jemma licked again, this time slowly, all the way from the base of my cock to the tip. "—this?"

I had to grip the sofa with both hands. This was so unbelievably hot. I could feel my cock was so hard it hurt. I had never gotten that hard from just one lick and a little gentle teasing before.

Jemma smiled as she made eye contact with me, then leaned in a little closer and opened her mouth. I couldn't wait to feel those lips around my cock. I watched as she closed her lips, moved her mouth away, quickly pulled my boxers back up, and stepped back. As I looked up at her, I saw the most mischievous smile flash across her face.

"Well, thank you, baby. I think that has answered all of my questions!" She gave the outline of my dick a gentle stroke before beginning to walk away.

"Hey!" I sprang up to my feet immediately, reaching out and grabbing her by the waist. "There's no way you can leave me like this?"

I was pointing at my rock-hard cock, just in case she didn't realize what I was talking about somehow. Perhaps I should add now I'm not some sort of cuckold with a tiny cock. I've watched enough cuckold porn to know that's a theme. Guys with tiny cocks. Well, that isn't me. I had a pretty decent-sized cock. A little longer than average and actually pretty thick. When I measured a while ago, it was 6 inches long but really quite girthy at just under 5.5 inches. I've never heard any complaints; in fact, usually the opposite. Almost all the women I've been with have said how much they love my thick cock. To be honest, the main issue at that moment was nothing to do with the size of my cock; it was to do with its state. It was so hard it physically hurt. This was all new to me. Jemma was usually a little more subdued when it came to sex, and as I said, she normally just took my lead. So seeing her take control like this and trying to work me up into a frenzy took my lust to another level entirely.

"Oh, babe, would you look at that!" She leaned forward just a little and planted a kiss right on the tip of my cock, through my boxers, where my precum was starting to create a dark wet spot on my boxers. "It looks like he really enjoyed the little show!"

I couldn't take any more of her teasing. I wanted her; I wanted her right then and there. I couldn't resist the urge any longer, and with that, I reached out and grabbed Jemma, then lifted her up and dropped her right down onto the couch. As soon as she hit the sofa, she giggled, almost as if she had anticipated it, biting her lip and lifting her gorgeous legs up toward the ceiling.

"Fuck me," she said in a deep, almost husky voice, so completely unlike her I had to do a double take to make sure it was my pretty little wife I was on top of on the sofa.

I wasted no time getting to work. I pulled her skirt and, a second later, slid her panties off, all the while kissing up her legs.

When I pushed her legs apart, I caught her looking right at me with the sexiest smirk on her face I'd ever seen. At that point, I knew I couldn't control myself any longer. I had slid my boxers down, and I had lined my cock up with her beautiful, clearly freshly shaved pussy and slid into her with no problem. I honestly think that was the wettest I've ever felt her. What followed was just a really hard fuck. Harder than we've ever fucked before, by far. There wasn't any niceness, any loving kisses. Just me on top of her, pinning her to the sofa and pounding away at her soaking wet pussy.

To say she was enjoying it was a massive understatement. Her wild moans only fueled the fire, and for the first time in our entire relationship, I felt her digging her nails into my back as we fucked, before she started to wrap her legs around my ass as if dragging me in, begging me to somehow fuck her even harder. It was truly unreal. When I felt like I was getting close to cumming, I lowered my head and whispered into her ear. "You're so wet, babe. I guess I'm not the only one who likes the idea."

I felt her legs grip around my back even harder and heard the word "fuck" escape her lips. A second later and her pussy started tightening around my cock. Jemma was cumming, and cumming hard. A few seconds of feeling her incredibly tight pussy cumming around my cock and I followed suit. It felt like I was cumming for 5 minutes like I was pumping a gallon of hot sticky cum inside her.

After that, we just lay there, gasping for air and holding each other on the couch. We weren't even fully undressed, so most of our clothes were soaked with sweat. I don't know if either of us had cum that quickly before. It was weird, we had probably just fucked for three or four minutes at the most, but it was the most incredible sex we had ever had, and I'm pretty sure that applied to both of us. At that moment, we didn't care for anything but fucking the living daylights out of each other.

"Holy fuck, babe, that was something else," Jemma said as she looked up at me and smiled with my arm draped over her shoulder.

Then we both started giggling and a few seconds later, we both just erupted in laughter.

Chapter 3

"Is it here?" Jemma asked as she stared at the map on her iPhone as I slowly drove down the rural road.

"I don't know, babe; you're the one looking at the map!" I chuckled as I said this; the most amusing part was that Jemma had refused to use the voice option on her phone at the start of the trip; it could have narrated the entire route for us. She insisted she would guide us the entire way through for some reason.

"Whatever. Turn left here." Jemma was zooming in and out on one section of her map, clearly getting increasingly frustrated. "I won't let this sultry Australian bitch on my phone replace me. No fucking way. My voice is the only one that gets to tell you what to do."

I turned into a small road framed by a canopy of large trees, their thick foliage letting through only thin slivers of sunlight to light up our path. It was actually pretty beautiful to see, so picturesque. I clearly was the only one who thought that way, as Jemma had already switched her phone to camera mode, documenting the path ahead.

"Uh, hold on, babe, what about the map? Are you sure you know where we're going from here?"

"Relax, babe. Don't worry," She said without looking up from her phone. "It's only a few more minutes; keep going straight ahead."

After we had been for lunch with our friends, Emma, Braun, Tasha, and her new boyfriend Karl, we all decided we would love to do a summer weekend Airbnb getaway outside the city. Personally, I loved the idea, as Jemma and I had been starting the feel the stresses and strains of work, and I think we both needed some rest and fresh inspiration. Now we were here, a month later, finally getting our wish.

But in the back of my mind, something was still bugging me. There was another topic, which we had shelved, that had originally come up right around the time we first started planning this mini vacation.

"Babe, urm......Do you remember when we were planning this trip?"

"Remember?" Jemma had put her phone in her pocket now, opting instead to hold my free hand.

I hesitated. I didn't want to fuck this up. "Do you remember the thing we talked about... the urm... the "cuckold" porn?"

She paused for a second before replying. "Yes. Yes, I do. What about it?"

"Well, we haven't really talked about it since. I mean, not properly. We just kind of got worked up and ended up having sex."

"Really great sex!"

"Yeah, really great sex!" I shifted a little in my seat, trying to get a little more comfortable. "So, what did you actually think about it? I've never seen you get so worked up like that before."

Again, she paused for a few seconds before responding. I could tell from her face she was a little embarrassed. "I... urm... I wanted to see if I could turn you on. I mean, when I watch porn... I normally only see really confident girls. It's like they own their sexuality. I feel like that's what makes it so hot."

"Yeah, I mean, I guess so." I struggled to find the words, something about being reminded that my innocent and usually so classy fiancée actually watches porn still had the power to stun me so completely. "Babe, you don't need to be like that. You fucking ooze sexiness, like always. You really don't have to act a particular way to turn me on. You're just fucking hot and turn me on. Period."

Jemma leaned into me and planted a gentle kiss on my cheek, and as she did, I felt her tongue licking me ever so slightly before as she pulled back. "You like that?"

We both giggled for a few seconds before she continued. "Thanks, babe. I love that I can turn you on, but honestly, that day was something else. You've never been that hard. You've never ever made love to me like that. You've never, ever done me that hard. I could tell it really, really got you going when I started to play up to your fantasy a little bit. As soon as

I acted a bit more confident and took the lead, you just kind of lost your shit, didn't you?"

"Yeah, I guess so." I paused for a second, took a deep breath, and swallowed some of my own confidence before continuing. "So babe, did you like the feeling too?"

I don't think, in all the time I've known Jemma, that I had ever seen her look as nervous as she did at that moment. She started fiddling with my fingers. "Yeah, I guess so. Yeah, I liked it a lot."

"But what about the fantasy, specifically?"

She didn't say anything at first, but I could feel her looking at me. "You mean me pretending to cuckold you? Or that I wanted to do it?"

I just remained quiet. I wanted her to get there on her own, and I think she knew the answer I was thinking. Yes, a thousand times yes.

"I mean... it was kind of fun to play along with it. But you don't really want to share me, honestly, do you?" She squeezed my hand a little tighter as she said it before leaning in for what I thought was another kiss. Instead, she moved her mouth against my ear and whispered, "Come on, babe, you know this little pussy is only for you, right?"

God, she was already irresistible, but this was like she had suddenly discovered another superpower. Sexual confidence. I never saw it coming, but I had wished it many times.

"Yeah," I mumbled, a very weak agreement from me.

It was like she sensed what I was feeling. "Babe, I know how much that kind of porn turns you on. I could tell that by how hard you were! I've never, ever felt a cock get that hard. Ever. But I really don't think I have the kind of confidence to...well, you know, perform? I don't think I could perform like that for you? The thing is, that's all it would ever be. It would be a performance. You're my guy, my fiancee, and I really don't think doing sexual stuff with another guy would actually get me going. Even the idea of it just feels wrong. It feels like I'd be cheating."

That was the longest explanation she had offered on the topic until that point, and although I didn't necessarily agree, I completely understood where she was coming from. If I'm honest, I wasn't even sure it was something I wanted to take further. I had the woman of my dreams, so why would I even consider sharing her with someone else? Would it be worth risking it just to fulfill my dirty fantasy? I knew that was kind of messed up. But despite all that, the idea of it had never really gone away, ever. I remained, just kind of lurking at the edges of my imagination. I couldn't deny that it turned me on enormously. Plus, perhaps she would be wrong about how it would feel if we ever tried it. I know for sure she was wetter than she's ever b—

"Right there! Oh, wow, it's huge!" Jemma was shouting a little as she pointed at a two-story house surrounded by an immaculately trimmed hedge on all sides. It was the perfect hideaway here in the countryside. There was also a car parked out front already, which was great. It meant we weren't the first ones to get here.

I parked up beside the car and turned the engine off. As I looked all around us, there was nothing but nature. Everywhere I looked, there was greenery, flowers, and some large decorative rocks all around us, as well as a brick house that looked like it had come straight out of a catalog for cozy homes as it stood there, sturdy and timeless.

"Wow, babe, this is exactly what we asked for, isn't it?" I said out loud as I continued looking around. "It's perfect, isn't it? Away from everything we know, and it looks like it's nice and private too?"

"You're right, babe; it looks perfect! Emma really knows how to pick 'em!" Jemma was already bounding for the trunk with a massive smile on her face. I popped the trunk for her, and we gathered our luggage and then excitedly made our way down the path to the front door.

As we got to the front door, we could see that it was pushed closed but hadn't shut properly or locked in any way, and Jemma just gently pushed it open. We then stepped into the entrance hall of the house. About a second after stepping in, we heard what sounded like something falling over, followed by hurried footsteps, which kind of surprised us.

Jemma and I looked at each other, completely confused, before Jemma yelled out, "Hello? Em? Tash?"

After a few more loud footsteps and sounds of some shuffling, we saw Tasha walk hurriedly into the entrance hallway we were in. "Hey, Jemma!" she said as she stopped right in the doorway. To say she looked disheveled would be the understatement of the century. Her hair was all over the place, her shirt was clearly on inside out, and that was all she seemed to be wearing. It was quite a long shirt, so I couldn't say for certain, but there definitely didn't look like there was anything on her bottom half, or at most just her underwear under the shirt. Jemma had grown up with Tasha; they were practically sisters. They were that close, so seeing her in that state probably wasn't a shocking sight for her, but it certainly was for me. I should add Tasha is a very attractive woman. Her dad is Asian, and her Mom is actually from Peru but was born in the USA, so she has a unique and very attractive quality about her. Her long, well, and immaculate black hair is down to her waist and she has legs that just seem to go on forever. Seeing her like that left me standing dumbfounded with my mouth open.

"Tasha!" Jemma squealed as she dropped her suitcase and ran to Tasha, hugging her best friend in the hallway as if she hadn't seen her in months. They both laughed a little, and I saw Jemma pull away a little before giggling as she said, "Girl, you smell like sex!"

Tasha's face instantly gave away how embarrassed she was as soon as Jemma said it. She pushed her away playfully and laughed. "What? No, I don't!?"

At that moment, another pair of hands emerged from the doorway and wrapped themselves around Tasha, and a second later, we could see Karl looking over her shoulder. He was Tasha's latest boyfriend or fling. With Tasha, it was honestly hard to say; she certainly went through a few. At the restaurant, he had introduced himself as an accountant working with high-profile clients, whatever that was supposed to mean. He was a little taller than me at 6 feet (I'm about 5'10"), and as he stepped in behind Tasha, I could see he hadn't bothered to put his shirt on, just a pair of sweatpants that didn't do much to hide the obvious bulge between his legs.

I figured Jemma's guess was correct. Emma and Braun must not be here yet, and these two had been taking full advantage of the empty house.

"Jemma! Good to see you again," Karl said as he released Tasha and stepped around her to hug Jemma. I raised an eyebrow at that. Was it really appropriate for a shirtless guy with a boner who had just been fucking Tasha to hug my fiancee? We barely knew this guy. But still, I figured he was just being polite.

"Oh, hi Karl," Jemma said, clearly uncomfortable as she backed away as soon as Karl's arms loosened.

Tasha came over to me and gave me a hug too. As soon as she stepped in close, I could immediately smell what Jemma was talking about. She smelled like a sweaty mess, but it wasn't just sweat; there was that distinctive smell, the one me and Jamma would often smell like after a particularly intense session. I ignored the smell, though, as it was nice to see Tasha in a different light. Ok, it was nice to see Tasha with so few clothes on! I also waved awkwardly toward Karl. "Hey, man."

"Hey dude, let me help you both with that!" He said, waving back at me as he approached the suitcase that Jemma had just dropped on the floor. As he walked toward it, I couldn't help but notice Karl was pretty jacked. I worked out a bit as well, and I wasn't in bad shape by any means, but Karl looked like he might have been a real gym rat. If I'm honest, it was slightly intimidating. His slicked-back blond hair, deep green eyes, and strong chin kind of made me think that Karl should have been a male model instead of an accountant. There was something about his looks and smug attitude that really rubbed me the wrong way. Today was no different. I was noticing all the same qualities in him again, which just brought the same feelings back. He was a total douchebag.

But this was a vacation. A trip away with friends to relax, so this wasn't time for an argument; it was time to focus on enjoying life.

"Right, shall we go inside then? This place is amazing!" Karl yelled this out as he walked alongside me while the girls were a few steps back. As they entered the doorway into the open-concept living area, Karl smiled and said, "Oh, and don't mind the clothes on the floor. Tash didn't have a chance to put them back on, so I lent her my shirt!"

I've never seen Tasha move so fast as she did to get to Karl and punch him on one of his oversized pecs. By this time, Jemma and Karl were laughing at Tasha's embarrassment as she made her way back to the front of the pack.

We got ourselves comfortable on the floor with its thick, plush carpet as Tasha and Karl sat on the sofa across from us. The sofa was made for two, maybe three at best, so we opted to settle down on the roomier carpet instead.

We were just about to call Emma and Braun to find out where they were, as they still hadn't arrived, and no one had heard from them. We needed to know as the sun had gone down, and we had even had our dinner, a filling takeout that Jemma and I had ordered just before we arrived and was delivered pretty quickly.

By now, everyone had showered and was in sleepwear now. It was that stage of the night where everyone was just kind of getting ready to chill out before bed. Karl had given us the grand tour around the house as him and Tasha had already explored it fully. I found it really strange that he felt he had to talk like a real estate agent who already knew the ins and outs of the building; after all, we were all new to the house! Anyway, the house was amazing and had three bedrooms upstairs, a washroom on both floors, and a beautiful spacious living room that shared space with a lovely little kitchen we could use. It was honestly a wonderful home. If it wasn't so far out from the city, it would be exactly the kind of house I'd want to buy. I could see myself living in long term if it was closer. But as it was, this was our home for the next two days.

Jemma picked up her phone and said she was calling Emma. As soon as she started speaking, a worried look plastered across her pretty face.

"Hey, Emma? Where are you guys!"

Jemma's eyes suddenly looked like they were ready to pop out of her head.

"An accident!? What? Where? Are you both alright? Fuck." Tasha sprang up as soon as she heard the word accident, and so did I. "Do you want us to come down there?"

A few moments of silence followed, and I should have suggested she put her phone on speaker. I was worried about my friends too.

"OK. But you're sure?" Jemma sat back down slowly as Tasha placed her hand on her shoulder. "Okay, well, as long as you're both alright. It's shit you guys won't be able to make it down here, though. You don't think you'll be able to get down, even for the day after?"

I sat down beside Jemma again. I was confused about what had gone on, but hearing that they were both fine was reassuring.

"Okay. Take care. Give my best to Braun too!"

Jemma put the phone down and looked just about ready to burst into tears. "They had a car accident as they were leaving the city. She said they're both okay, but they need to get the car repaired, and Braun has got some serious whiplash. They're just trying to play it safe by staying in the city." Jemma frowned as she told us this.

"Oh shit," Tasha said, with a worried look on her face, and then looked at Karl. "Do you think we should head back tomorrow? To check on them?"

"No, no," Jemma said as she put away her phone and squeezed up next to me. "Emma said they were fine and told me to enjoy the place. We all paid for it, and she said she didn't want it going to waste."

Tasha nodded and then slowly made her way to the sofa before she sat down and turned on the TV. She logged into Netflix and started scrolling through the options until she stopped on Home Alone.

"Tash, come on, babe, everyone knows that's a Christmas Movie!" Jemma pointed out, perking up a little.

"No, it's not a Christmas movie; it's a feel-good movie!" Tasha replied as she broke out into one of her trademark pouts as she crossed her arms. "Karl, back me up!"

Karl let out a boisterous laugh before nodding his agreement. "I'm down, Tash. But don't worry, we can make it interesting."

He reached over the end of the sofa and grabbed a rucksack from the floor. As he pulled it up onto his lap, Karl quickly unzipped it and, a second later, pulled out what looked to be a bottle of Jack and some cans of Red Bull. "I brought a little alcohol and mix. Bought enough for six! Now as Emma said, we can't let this go to waste, can we?"

Tasha's eyes lit up. "Home Alone... Drinking Game!" She squeezed right up to Karl, and her eyes looked like an excited koala, tightly wrapping her limbs around Karl. To his credit, Karl played the part of the sturdy tree pretty well.

We all just laughed as we decided to make the most of our first night here. We were going to have fun, for Emma and Braun.

Chapter 4

"Shots!" Karl yelled out, as on screen, a shovel smacked the unfortunate Marv in the face, followed by smashing Harry in the face as well. "Shots again!"

Jemma, Tasha, and I chugged down our shots which we were drinking out of small red cups Karl had used to pour them. Karl had downed far more drinks than the three of us so far. He was drinking extra shots in the moments between the shots we were supposed to be taking. Still, despite the extra alcohol, he seemed completely unphased. He was clearly capable of holding his drink. It was shot for every time someone got hurt, and toward the end of Home Alone, Harry and Marv get hurt a lot! Every shovel in the face was another shot.

As the film wound down, the girls both snuggled up closer to the guys, and with the warmth of our bodies and the room, we were starting to feel nice and snug. It was really cozy and rather nice. Maybe the weekend wouldn't be a complete waste after all, despite Emma and Braun having to cancel at the last minute. I looked down at my beautiful fiancée, and I could see her face was a little flushed from all the drinking. She never could handle her drink. As I looked down, she looked back up at me, and it didn't take long for it to turn into a peck. And then that brief peck turned into a full-on kiss.

We eventually had to stop when Tasha and Karl began to hoot and holler. Jemma quickly pulled away, pretty embarrassed. She definitely wasn't normally the type to show any sort of affection in public, let alone a proper passionate kiss. But clearly, the alcohol had lowered her inhibitions, and she was much more willing to push her usual boundaries. I certainly didn't consider it a problem, though.

"Well, I think that's us guys. I think it's time we turn in," Tasha remarked, her cheeks looking pretty rosy. "We've got a lot of fun to get ready for tomorrow!" As she said this, she turned to Karl and whispered just loud enough for me and Jemma to hear, "Oh, and a lot of fun left to have tonight."

Karl laughed as she said this and planted a sloppy kiss on Tasha's lips. "Come on, baby! The night's still young. Let's play one more game."

"What game do you want to play?" Jemma's face gave away that she was genuinely curious. She took my arms and wrapped them around herself. "We don't have any cards, so we can't play a card game!"

Karl smirked as he reached into the now-empty duffel bag, and after a few seconds, he smiled. "Well, that is if I haven't lost it... Ah, there it is!" When Karl removed his hand from the bag, he was holding a die.

"What's that for? There aren't any real drinking games you can play with dice." I heard my voice and realized I was sounding a bit slurred. I took a deep breath and did my best to hide it as I continued to speak.

Without saying another word, he threw the die over to us. As soon as I looked at it, the game was obvious. There were no numbers on any of the faces of this die. Just words: kiss, touch, suck, blow, lick, and a question mark. I'd seen these before on Instagram, but I've never actually had a chance to try it out myself.

"Don't they usually come in pairs?" I asked. I was pretty sure that the other die in the pair usually listed the body parts on which the acts were to be performed.

"Yeah!" Karl laughed out loud. I hated his laugh. It irritated me every time he laughed. "I can't find the other one, so I figured we could just let the person who rolls decide on their own!"

I looked at Jemma, and although she seemed a bit drunk, she was smiling. My normally innocent and conservative fiance seemed like she was okay with the game. I actually thought it might be pretty fun as well. If I'm honest, I definitely wasn't thinking anything through properly by this point. "Ok, let's give it a go. It sounds like fun."

Tasha pouted a little bit as she said, "Ugh, but babe, it's time to go upstairs, booo." I could see her biting her lips at this point as her hand squeezed Karl's thigh.

Karl returned the look with a kiss as he smiled and said, "Oh, come on, babe, just a little bit of fun down here first?"

Tasha kept the pout going, but now she had put her hand out in my direction. "Ok, but I'm starting to get sleepy. Give me the dice." With that, I handed her the dice, stepped back, and said, "Good luck!"

While Tasha looked at the dice, I decided to push my luck slightly and started to get a little handsy with Jemma. I slid my hand across her boob and brushed her nipples a little. I could barely feel it through her top, but I could feel it. I couldn't say for sure, but it felt hard. Perhaps it was just the brushing that caused the reaction.

Me and Jemma aren't big drinkers normally, so we don't usually get drunk when it's just the two of us. As we sat there feeling the effects of the drink, I was starting to get a little turned on thinking about what we might do once we went upstairs. A second later, when I felt Jemma sneak her hand behind her back and start gently stroking it over my crotch, I knew my beautiful fiancée was feeling the exact same way.

"Right, so what do I do now?" Tasha asked as she rolled the die.

"Quick, name a body part!" Karl shouted. "Quickly!"

"Huh? Urm.... Tongue? Fuck, I don't know."

The die stopped, and we all looked. It had landed on "blow." Jemma, Karl, and I all instantly started laughing.

"How the fuck do you blow a tongue!?" I was almost in tears at the thought, and Jemma was just giggling next to me.

"Ugh. Who? Whose tongue are we talking about?" Tasha furrowed her brow as she asked. I could kind of tell why she pouted and frowned so much. It was genuinely very cute, and a part of me actually felt sympathy for her. I guess that was her superpower!

Karl reached out and handed her an empty beer bottle he had finished earlier in the evening between some shots. "Spin it and find out!"

Tasha begrudgingly placed the bottle on the floor in the gap between the four of us. I could tell straight away that there was too much friction from the carpet, and the bottle wouldn't spin properly. I was right as it weakly spun around just once, stopping to point at Jemma's feet. Jemma quickly pulled her feet away and let out a little scream. It was adorable to watch as she put both hands up to cover her face.

Tasha grinned when she saw this and crept closer to Jemma. "Oh Jemma, Tasha's here to blow your sexy little tongue."

Jemma couldn't help but start giggling as Tasha gently pulled her hands from her face. "Ready?"

Fuck. That's kind of hot.

Karl and I had fallen silent at this point. I guess it would have been obvious to anyone watching that we were both eagerly anticipating how this would go down. I didn't know how Jemma was going to react, but I wanted to find out.

Jemma nodded at Tasha, who was clearly more than ready to take the lead. "Tongue. Out. Now." Jemma blushed deeply as Tasha ordered her around, but her tongue slid out a second later without any resistance. She just sat there with her little tongue sticking out in Tasha's face.

Tasha then slowly moved in, bringing her lips closer to Jemma's tongue before sliding it into her mouth. As soon as Tasha's mouth closed around her tongue, Jemma's eyes shot open. Her face gave away how shocked she was as Tasha started to work on her tongue. It became pretty clear that Tasha interpreted the "blow" action on the die as "give a blowjob," and she was now moving her mouth up and down, giving Jemma's tongue the blowjob of its life. A lot of different thoughts ran through my mind at that point. Firstly, Tasha has clearly got a very good blowjob technique; secondly, Jemma's tongue is actually pretty solid to withstand such a sucking; and thirdly, Jemma seemed absolutely OK with it.

After about 10 or 15 seconds of Jemma having her tongue sucked exactly like it was a cock something changed. I couldn't even say who started it, but the two girls came together more and more. Jemma's tongue started withdrawing back into her mouth, and Tasha's mouth closed the distance. Before any of us knew what was happening, it had turned into the two of them making out. And this wasn't just the sort of little makeout show drunk girls do for the boys sometimes. I was pretty shocked to watch as my drunk fiancée shut her eyes and slid her hand up to the side of Tasha's face. Holy fuck, I thought to myself, Jemma is enjoying this way more than I expected.

When Tasha finally pulled away, Karl started whooping from where he was sitting. "Yeah, That's my girl!"

I slid closer to her and held Jemma tight once the kiss had ended. She had already gone back to covering her face from embarrassment. "That was fucking hot," I whispered to her.

"What!? That? Come on, babe, I'm a terrible kisser, and I've never even kissed another girl before!" She whispered back.

I gave her a peck on the cheek and smiled to reassure her.

As I looked over, I saw that Karl and Tasha had also shared a peck and then some. They seemed to be entirely in their own little world as they started making out.

"That was so hot, Tash," Karl smirked at Tasha and then over at Jemma. "Jemma, I'm not gonna lie. You taste damn good!"

I was a bit taken aback by this comment.

I guess we were all drunk, and a bit of friendly joking around was okay, but hearing him say that my fiance tasted good was a bit of a shock, to say the least. I looked down at Jemma; by now, she was just full-on covering her face, hiding from sight, so I decided to let that comment go.

However, as much as his comment irritated me, something else was happening, something odd. As I felt myself getting angry at Karl's comment, I could also feel my cock getting hard, and with how we were positioned, it was definitely poking into Jemma's back. She hadn't reacted to it, so I kind of hoped she would just let it go. I was pretty sure it was caused by what Tasha just did. Watching her kiss my pretty fiance was enough to get any guy hard, surely? It just happened that Karl was being a douchebag and making those comments at the same time. It wasn't anything to do with him.

Tasha smacked Karl in the chest as he made that comment, although it was more of a playful slap than anything; as soon as she did it, she kissed him quickly afterward.

"Right babe, Jemma, it's your turn!" Tasha managed to get out between kisses.

Jemma looked at the die and bottle on the floor and then up at me. "Babe, do you think this is okay?"

"Of course it is," Karl answered. That really annoyed me. Jemma clearly wasn't talking to him. What the fuck made him feel like it was okay to answer for me? "He's fine; come on, just look at him. He enjoyed watching just as much as you did taking part! Fuck it, I know I did."

Jemma looked at me without saying another word, then reached her arm out for the die hesitantly. She picked it up, took a deep breath, then sat up straight and rolled it. As she eased back down, she pressed up against my erection. Before either of us knew what was happening, she let out a loud whisper. "Hard cock?"

Normally she would never just say that out loud, where other people could hear. But I guess the mixture of the alcohol, genuine curiosity, and the atmosphere just got to her, and something happened. And the way it all just came together, her mind was thinking she needed to say a body part, she was probably willing herself to say one out loud and then she felt my hard cock and the words just came out.

My head jolted up to look at Karl and Tasha, desperately hoping they hadn't heard. Well, the excited gasps as they looked at the die gave it away that they had heard Jemma's little slip-up. The die landed on "touch."

Jemma went bright red as she saw it. "Wait, shit. No, I was just talking to Rich about—"

"Cock?" Karl interrupted. "Yeah, that's right. We all heard you clearly say cock. Now you've got to deal with the consequences! You better hope it lands on Rich!" Karl handed Jemma the bottle as he said this.

Jemma took the bottle from him and looked at me with a worried look on her face.

"Don't worry, Jemma. If it points to me, you can just touch me down there. It won't be as bad as what we just did," Tasha said while giving Jemma a naughty wink.

For some reason, that little comment seemed to calm Jemma down a little because she smiled weakly and spun the bottle.

Looking back now, I know that was the moment I should have called a stop to the game. That was the chance to stop it before it got serious. But for whatever reason, I didn't. I just sat and watched as the madness marched on.

My voice caught in my throat as I saw where the bottle had stopped. Karl was already laughing and celebrating like his team had just won the Superbowl. He actually jumped up from the carpet. Weirdly, Tasha didn't seem to mind too much. For whatever reason, she didn't seem to care that her boyfriend was over the moon about having another woman touch his hard cock. She just sat there pouting at Jemma. "Maybe next time you can be that excited if it's the two of us?" Tasha almost growled at Karl before she playfully punched his leg. "Don't get yourself too excited now!"

Jemma looked up at me, the worry clear from her face. As she leaned against me, she felt the thing that had got her in this trouble and raised an eyebrow. My cock was rock hard, as hard as it had ever been. Probably as hard as the night we talked about my fantasies, and as much as I really hated Karl, I was starting to understand why this entire situation was turning me on so much.

"Hey, Jemma. I'm waiting, baby!" Karl was standing up now and was unzipping his pants as he smiled at Jemma. His smugness was really pissing me off, but I sort of accepted that we agreed to play the game, and there were rules. At least, that's what I kept thinking to myself. Jemma and I had talked about my weird fetish before, but the way that ended, I never thought it would go anywhere. Then suddenly, this happened. Suddenly we were all a little drunk, and Jenna had just been kissed by Tasah, and now, well, this was a whole new level entirely. That was definitely not lost on me.

Jemma seemed to pick up on this. As she slowly started crawling over to where Karl had now sat down, she looked at me, confused. Before I could say or do anything, Tasha spoke. "Don't worry, Jem, it's really nothing special."

Karl just ignored his girlfriend's comment and continued to unbuckle his pants. Jemma was now sitting between me and Karl, in a position that blocked my view completely. As I looked up, Tasha had clearly picked up on this right away. "Hey Rich, you want to move closer?"

It felt like I was really put on the spot at that moment. My gut reaction was to shake my head and deny it. To tell them I didn't want to watch my pretty little fiance touch another guy's hard cock. Plus, I didn't want this asshole to think I wanted to see his cock.

"Why would he want to see it?" Karl asked. As he said that, he stopped shifting around, and I saw his arm move, and it was obvious he had just slipped his cock out of his pants. God, what I'd give to have a better view.

I couldn't see Jemma's reaction as he got it out, but Karl instantly piped up. "Impressive, right? Now just wrap your hand around it... if you can get it round it."

I watched as Tasha rolled her eyes beside him.

At this point, I hadn't heard a word from Jemma, but I could see her right arm was moving.

"Yeah, that's right, there you go, Jemma. Come on, it feels good right?"

What the fuck. Karl was such an intolerable prick! Sure, we had to stick to the rules of the game. Touch and hard penis, and the bottle picked him out. But he didn't have to be such a smug cunt about it.

Chapter 5

At that moment, I knew for sure that I should never have let this get this far. I know Jemma would have stopped the moment I said I was uncomfortable with anything, but I didn't say anything. And now she was touching that asshole's cock! But the worst part, even worse than the fact it was Karl, a guy I really couldn't stand, was the fact that it was turning me on beyond reason. I was now having to do some pretty extreme shifting around to hide my erection. I wanted nothing more than to see my fiancée's delicate little fingers wrapped around another man's cock. Or, at the very least, to be able to get my own cock out and start stroking it. I was so turned on and hard it was actually hurting my cock! But I knew deep down that the right thing to do at that moment was to just sit and wait. Not to do anything that might embarrass myself or Jemma.

I could take some time and process all these emotions later.

Then, without any warning, Jemma pulled back, turned away from Karl, and crawled towards me. I could see that she was blushing from ear to ear, a deep red that I had never seen her go before.

"Well, I guess we're all having fun now!" Karl yelled out, chuckling as he pulled up his pants. I was so distracted by Jemma, who seemed to need my attention, that I didn't even catch a sight of the supposedly thick cock she had just had her hands on. By the time I looked up, Karl had put his cock away.

Tasha yawned, then grabbed the die and bottle and pushed them toward me. "Come on, let's go! I need to get my beauty sleep!"

I had my arm around Jemma again, but now it seemed like she was actively hiding her face from me, not anyone else. Was she okay? How was she feeling right now? I really wanted to know.

I grabbed the die and bottle, and Jemma didn't move. She just lay there with her back up against me. I couldn't see her facial expression, but I could see that asshole Karl staring at her though. He wasn't egging me on, so I knew he must be distracted by something. Well, by Jemma. By now, a huge part of me really wanted the bottle to stop, as it pointed at Tasha. Then I could give Karl a taste of his own medicine, and obviously, a tiny little part of me wouldn't have minded at all getting to play with Tasha.

The more I thought about it, the more I realized it actually wasn't a bad idea at all. I figured that with the carpet, it really wouldn't be too hard to spin the bottle and make it stop where I wanted it to. The carpet was catching pretty easily, so I knew with the right amount of power...

I took a deep breath and rolled the die. I immediately shouted 'BOOBS' to which Tasha and Karl started laughing. That laughter turned to "ooh's" as they saw the die had landed on "suck."

Then it was time to spin the bottle. I took another deep breath and got the bottle pointing right where I wanted it. I gave it a spin, just enough power to cause one full spin, and just as I had planned, the bottle took one spin before slowly stopping, pointing at Tasha.

I tried my best to look casual, but I don't think it worked too well, as a second later, Jemma looked up at me and playfully slapped my arm while frowning at me. I could see Karl and Tasha talking to each other in hushed voices out of the corner of my eye as I did my best to reassure Jemma with a smile.

"Okay, okay, fuck it, let's get it over and done with," Karl smirked. "It's only fair, I guess!"

A second later, he slid himself behind Tasha with surprising speed, and before I knew it, he had pulled her shirt up. Tasha was clearly shocked as well, as her arms were pulled upwards suddenly from the motion causing her perky breasts to pop out of her bra and into view. I had to stop myself from staring with my mouth open. Tasha's tits weren't big at all. They were smaller than Jemma's; I'd guess they were an A cup. Jemma isn't exactly busty, and she's a b-cups and clearly bigger than Tasha. But even though they were small, Tasha's perky breasts were still a massive turn-on. The nipples were beautiful. Small, dark, rock hard, and her breasts were so firm it was unreal. Karl had continued to slide Tasha's shirt up her arms, so she now had her hands up above her head with her shirt around her wrists, trapping her arms. She was now sitting there, unable to move and unable to cover herself up! The prick was actually exposing his girlfriend like this.

"Well? They're nice, aren't they?"

What the fuck, Karl!" Tasha was glaring up at him, but despite the anger in her voice and the embarrassed look on her face, she was doing absolutely nothing to resist. She could have struggled free, I'm sure of it. Then she turned her head to look at me, and with the slightest hint of a smile, she said, "Be gentle; they're very sensitive."

I could see that Jemma was watching as well, but I really couldn't read her face. There was just a bit of a blank expression. Then she leaned forward and said, "Now, baby, don't go getting too into it, OK." Jemma wasn't looking at me when she said it, and I could tell by her tone that she wasn't entirely keen on the prospect of me sucking her friend's tits. But then I could see she was thinking it through hard. It was like she knew she didn't like the idea but knew it was only fair. After all, she had just had her hands on Karl's cock!

I've always thought Tasha was incredibly hot. I might never have said it to Jenna in those terms, but it was true. I'd always left it as a "yeah, Tasha's cute; I can see why guys like her. She's not really my type, though." I never liked lying to Jemma, but what was I meant to say? "Fuck babe, your best friend would be a solid 10 if she had some tits?" Imagine how that would have gone down?

As much as I've always fancied Tasha, the main point of this little plan was to get some sort of revenge on Karl for his earlier antics with Jemma, but his enthusiasm about the whole thing was making me question if my initial plan to get him jealous was going to have any effect at all. It really wasn't the reaction I expected at all. It was almost like he wanted me to suck Tasha's tits. On top of that, it really didn't seem like Jemma was up for me doing it. She really didn't seem comfortable with the thought of my mouth on Tasha's tits. But she had only just touched Karl's cock, so surely this was only fair?

I gently moved out from behind Jemma and shuffled over to where Tasha was sitting, with her tits exposed. As I got closer, I could see her nipples were still getting harder, and it looked like she was desperately trying to hide her embarrassment, trying to hold her gaze on the blank television screen.

I didn't even want to look at Karl because I knew seeing his stupid face would just ruin the moment for me. I didn't want the last thing I saw before I felt Tasha's beautiful nipples to be his stupid face. I took a breath in as I leaned forward and approached Tasha. I was determined to just enjoy this for what it was, a chance to suck a hot girl's little tits. With that thought, I closed my mouth around her right nipple and started to suck. I closed my eyes as I began to suck; her nipple was rock hard and so sensitive I could feel it react instantly. Then a second later, I heard her start moaning. I was stunned and pulled away. It was a seriously hot moment for me, but I really didn't expect her to react in that way. And I definitely didn't expect her to react so loudly. She didn't say a word and just continued to look at the screen until Karl finally released her hands from her shirt, which he did by sliding her shirt completely off as he pulled away.

"Fuck off, Karl," Tasha screamed as she grabbed her breasts and covered them as best she could with her arms while she glared at Karl. "I've had enough of your bullshit. I'm going to bed now, Karl. Come upstairs when you're done, and bring my fucking shirt." With that, the angry and extremely pouty Tasha stood up and walked off upstairs.

"Don't you mean my shirt?" Karl roared at her as she climbed the stairs, but Tasha just ignored him. He looked back over toward us instead and said, "Well, let's finish up the game before I have to go console her."

I paused for a second and stared at him. I was confused. What needed finishing up? I'd just sucked his girlfriend's tit in front of him; he'd had my fiance's hand on his cock. I snapped, "Tasha's just left. I think the game's pretty much done." It was the first time I'd lost my patience with him all night, and I can't deny it felt good.

"No, babe, fair is fair. Karl never got a turn on the dice." Jemma piped up, which I was surprised by. It had already been a night full of firsts, and knowing Jemma, I was surprised she wanted it to continue. Though from looking at her face, I could see she seemed a bit annoyed. I guess I deserved that.

"That's what I like to hear!" Karl said as he ran over and picked up the die and the bottle, then took a seat on the couch instead of the carpet. "Ready? The body part is "all over"! As in, well, you know, everywhere!"

I slowly sat down as he spoke, but I caught a look from Karl, and he smiled and then winked at me. Did he really just wink at me? I saw Karl lower the bottle onto the carpet, and then spin it, almost exactly like I had done when it landed on Tasha. I knew where it was going to stop before it stopped. The bottle was pointing straight at Jemma.

"W-wait." Jemma looked a little bit concerned now. "You didn't even roll the die!"

"Oh, oops," Karl said with a smile as he quickly rolled the dice, purposely launching it in Jemma's direction. "What does it say, Jemma?"

Jemma looked down at the die and looked mortified as she looked back up at me and then over at Karl before saying meekly, "Kiss."

I felt myself shifting uncomfortably in the seat as the realization of what was about to happen dawned on me, but worst of all, I was starting to feel the first stirrings of another boner. This wasn't right at all. Karl knew where that bottle was going to stop, and I should have called him out and stopped the game. Jemma didn't need to do this.

Those thoughts were soon overtaken by some rather intense emotions. I really wanted to put a stop to this, but I couldn't. It was the same sensation of my voice being caught in my throat that I'd felt only a few minutes ago. As much as I wanted to put a stop to this, there was a part of me that wanted to see this through. So I did nothing. I just sat there frozen as Jemma looked nervously toward me.

"Well, come on, Jemma, what are you waiting for? Let's finish this up! Tasha's waiting." With that, Karl stood up and, with a smug grin on his face, motioned toward the couch. "Your throne awaits, my queen."

Jemma slowly made her way over to the couch and sat down awkwardly in front of Karl. She looked more nervous than I'd ever seen her before, and she couldn't sit still as she kept trying to shift away from Karl's prying eyes.

"Do we really want to go through with this?" she asked me while she slid along the couch, trying to slide as far away from Karl as possible. I gave her a blank look back. I knew she had a point. I was completely unsure if I really wanted this to go ahead. Was this like forbidden fruit, something better left to the imagination? But then I also knew that I had just done the exact same bottle trick to get it to stop on Tasha, and I could have said no to sucking her tits, but I didn't.

Jemma just kept looking at me as if waiting for me to stop the game, but it was well past that point now. Karl didn't want to wait any longer. He inched closer to Jemma, moving slowly so that he didn't spook her while she held her gaze with me. Karl could barely hide the excitement on his face as he slowly closed the gap between them.

Finally, I slowly nodded at Jemma, who mirrored my nod back, just as Karl gently started nibbling against her tender neck. He actually moaned out loud as he started to explore her neck with his mouth. But the worst part wasn't that Karl was enjoying it; that was to be expected. The worst part was that Jemma closed her eyes and seemed to shiver from head to toe as he kissed her neck.

A part of her was clearly enjoying this. Part of her clearly enjoyed being put on a pedestal by her fiancé and another guy, but it was like she didn't want to surrender completely. Not yet. She was still my fiance.

"Karl, wait, I.....aaah fuck......Karl, wait........" But Jemma's weak protests fell on deaf ears. Karl was relentless with his mouth as he pored over every inch of her neck and collarbone, towering over her as he planted kisses on her sensitive neck.

I was stunned. I felt like I was in shock.

The sweatpants I was wearing helped hide how much I was enjoying it all because, as I looked down, my cock was somehow already fully hard. I don't think I'd ever got a hard-on quite so quick in all my life. In fact, I'm pretty sure I could have blown my load right then and there if it wasn't for my own disbelief that this was actually happening. Before tonight, Jemma has never shown even the slightest hint of interest in Karl. In fact, since we'd been together, she had never shown even the hit of interest in any other guy. So sitting there watching her close her eyes and her body respond to Karl kissing her neck was setting off fireworks in my brain.

Jemma still looked at me whenever she opened her eyes, and she still had that expression, a mixture of shock and confusion on her pretty face as Karl continued to plant kisses all over her. But as I watched, something was starting to make me feel a little unsettled. As much as watching Karl's mouth on Jemma's neck was turning me on, something about it was starting to make me feel sick. It wasn't what Karl was doing with his mouth; it wasn't even that I was pretty sure he was going to take his mouth to other places. What made me feel sick was the way Jemma was slowly tilting her neck back. It was like she was inviting more of Karl's advances. She wanted this. She wasn't doing this for me, to indulge my fantasy. She was doing this because she wanted Karl to kiss her neck.

But as much as I felt sick watching her react so keenly to Karl's touch, there was no way I could deny it was turning me on an insane amount as well. It was so much hotter than any cuckold or hotwife porn I'd ever watched before. It was my fiance as the porn star, and I was lucky enough to have front-row seats.

As I watched, I could see Jemma's earlier hesitance and defenses slowly starting to break down. Perhaps she remembered our earlier conversations and that this was all part of my fantasy I had wanted to explore. Maybe she thought this might be something we could enjoy together if she could just find a way to let go.

And slowly, right in front of me, that was exactly what she did.

After another minute or two of Karl's mouth pleasuring her neck, I watched as she bit her lip and allowed the pleasure and illicit nature of the entire situation to take over. She let out a moan and laid back completely against the couch. Her body was no longer offering any resistance at all. She was allowing Karl to do what he wanted.

I know I should have been angry. Hell, I should have got up and tackled Karl right then and there. He had gone well past the boundaries of the game. I sucked Tasha's tits for a few seconds because that's how the game works. He was no longer playing the game. He was engaged in foreplay with my fiance, and I was sitting there watching it. But as much as one part of me hated it, I knew this was exactly what Jemma and I had talked about. I couldn't screw this up now. This could be my only chance to ever experience this fantasy. I'd never imagined it could even get this far, and now Jemma was not running for the hills; I knew it was my best shot.

So instead of saying anything, instead of stopping Karl from going further with my fiance, I did something that shocked even me. I just sat there and slid my hand down inside my pants, reaching for my cock. As soon as I felt it, I could tell it was rock-hard and desperately begging for attention. I started to stroke my cock, slowly. Seeing my fiancée in this situation was far hotter than I could have ever imagined, and the last thing I wanted to do was blow my load now. That would have been so embarrassing.

By now, Jemma's eyes were completely shit, and her hands gripped the couch in silent protest. As I watched her, I could see from her face that the feelings of desire she had been keeping at bay were slowly bubbling to the surface.

Karl seemed to notice this as well. A few seconds later, he started to take off his top, once again revealing his chiseled torso. I'm not sure if Jemma had even noticed he had taken his top off at that point, but she definitely did a second later as he started to try and remove her top.

Her eyes shot open instantly, and she looked at me again with a look of pleading in her eyes. I couldn't tell if she was pleading with me to stop this or pleading with me to give her permission to carry on. But in the end, it didn't matter. A few seconds later, she raised her own hands in the air, allowing the very eager Karl to slide her thin shirt straight over her head without a struggle.

Her little bra was now the only item of clothing covering Jemma's upper body. Her toned stomach was now completely exposed as her bra just about hid her perky boobs. To my surprise, and probably Jemma's, Karl completely ignored Jemma's boobs. He started planting kisses all over Jemma's stomach, then started to move his kisses down toward her sweatpants. I could see her knuckles turning white from how hard she was gripping the cushions. She turned her head to face me once again, and I could see from her eyes how embarrassed she was. She must have been embarrassed that another man was having this effect on her, and I was embarrassed that I was just sitting there, enjoying it and doing nothing about it.

Then Karl moved his face even lower. He was now kissing her thighs through the sweatpants, and I was just watching another man's head buried between her legs. Well, I say just watching. I wasn't just watching at all. I was watching with my hand down my pants, stroking my swollen cock. Jemma's face was bright red now as fear and embarrassment had taken over. We locked eyes, and I knew she was having doubts.

Chapter 6

I took a deep breath in. I knew this was the point of no return.

"Oh fuck, babe... I really don't know..." she whispered as her eyes darted from me and then back to Karl. Her eyes fixed back onto Karl, who was now kissing the top of her thighs through her sweatpants. His mouth was literally a few layers from her pussy.

Before I could say a word, Karl's hands slid up to the waistband of Jemma's sweatpants and gripped tight. I could see that he had also grabbed onto her the waistband of her panties. Jemma's eyes shot wide open as a look of sheer panic spread across her face. Her hands immediately grabbed hold of Karl's hands, desperate to stop him from ripping her last bits of decency right off.

"What's up, babe?" Karl asked, looking genuinely confused but with the same stupid grin on his face. "Come on, it's all part of the game!"

Jemma looked over toward me once more, and by now, she was looking genuinely terrified. "Babe, I really don't know if I can do this."

Her adorable expression managed to tug at every one of my heartstrings. In fact, the look she gave me had such an impact that I stood up and walked over. It felt weird; it felt like I wasn't in full control of what I was doing, like some weird out-of-body experience, as I took a few slow steps and propped myself up on my knees next to her on the couch. I leaned in and gently kissed her on the lips in an effort to console my clearly troubled and half-naked fiancée.

You know those moments where your body somehow moves before you even will it to? Well, this was one of those moments. And despite all her anxiety and worry, this was undoubtedly one of the best kisses I had ever shared with Jemma. I could feel my cock twitch as our tongues started dancing around each other.

The kiss was so good I must have actually closed my eyes because I was taken by complete surprise when Jemma let out a little yelp. I opened my eyes instantly, and as soon as I looked down, I saw Karl with that same shit-eating grin on his face as he slid Jemma's sweatpants down her shins and dragged them and her underwear off her legs completely. Jemma's little shaved pussy was exposed to another guy for the first time in years. As I looked at Jemma, I saw her hands were down by her side, limp. It was like she had thrown everything into that kiss to take her mind off of exactly what was happening, and it had worked. However, I was very much in the moment, and my God, what an intense moment it was. Things had just progressed an insane amount in a few short seconds, and somehow things were still hotting up.

Before I could say anything, Karl just smiled and said, "Jackpot," as he buried his face straight down into my fiancée's exposed pussy. Jemma's eyes jolted open again, and her whole body tensed up visibly as she stared down at Karl. He looked up at her briefly, but after shooting her a quick smile, he moved his face further up, and I saw him open his mouth. I knew he was about to lick my fiance's pussy. I knew his tongue was about to do something that had been reserved for me and me alone for many years. He was about to do something me and Jemma both absolutely loved. Well, I loved it when I was the one doing it.

Jemma's mouth was now wide open in complete shock as Karl's tongue made contact with her sensitive pussy. Her whole body was still incredibly tense, and her hands gripped the couch again like her life depended on it as she stared down at Karl. However, Karl wasn't looking up at her anymore; he was thoroughly occupied. I could tell instantly that Karl was a confident pussy licker, and he moved his arm into a position that I knew meant he was going to try and get some fingers to work alongside his tongue. He must have been licking Jemma's pussy for five seconds before she finally relaxed enough to speak.

She bit down hard on her lip with a look of total confusion on her face, "Stop, Karl, please. Oh fuck. Karl, seriously. This isn't part of the game. Please, fuck oh god, stop Karl, please."

I could feel Jemma's whole body trembling in my arms. Holy fuck! Karl knew what he was doing when it came to licking pussy; that much was obvious.

Watching Karl's head disappear between my fiance's thighs was an incredible sight. There was something so visceral, so brutal about seeing it. But however powerful the sight was, the physical feeling was even more powerful. Holding Jemma and feeling her entire body shook with anticipation and pleasure was something I will never be able to put into words.

Karl had only been down there a few seconds, but I just couldn't take it anymore. I knew my cock had been just about ready to explode ages ago; now, it was so hard it actually hurt. I couldn't resist any longer, and with that thought, I pulled down my sweatpants and allowed my cock to spring out. Almost instantly, Jemma turned her head to that side, and unintentionally, my cock slapped against her face, causing her to look up in shock at me.

"What the fuck, babe?" was all she said before she groaned again as Karl's tongue clearly hit a pleasurable spot.

I stared down at Jemma, hopeful that the look of desperation on my face was enough of a clue for her to understand what I wanted. As our eyes met, Jemma looked absolutely incredulous. A second later and Karl also looked up to see what was going on, but he just saw my cock and went straight back to working on Jemma's pussy with his mouth. Jenna's eyes closed again, and I realized there was no chance of getting my cock in her mouth; Karl was distracting her far too much.

But then something incredible happened. Without opening her eyes, my beautiful fiancée started to open her lips, and a second later, she moved her mouth toward my cock. I didn't need a second invitation, and I pushed my hips forward slightly, just enough to guide the tip of my cock into her mouth. As soon as her lips closed around the tip of my cock I was in heaven. This whole scene had been unthinkable not too long ago.

But now, somehow, I had my sexy fiancée almost completely naked, well, bottomless, wearing just a bra. The fact she still had her bra on somehow made it worse as she was sandwiched between me and another man. She was being pleasured while she slowly sucked me off. This was an unbelievably intoxicating blend. I genuinely can't explain in words how incredible this felt. It was like I didn't know if I was more likely to pass out or wake up.

Karl looked up at us again as he must have heard my moans as Jemma started sucking my cock. When he saw what she was doing, we made eye contact, and he just smiled before he went back to work. I think that was the point where all three of us accepted we were well past the point of no return now. All that was left for us to do was to enjoy the moment.

Running on instinct, I slid my hand down, unclasped the back of Jemma's bra, and slid it off her shoulders, freeing her perky little tits. Her nipples looked absolutely stunning, as hard as I've ever seen, and really dark red. For a second, she pulled my cock out of her mouth and looked up at me.

"What the fuck are you doing?" she asked.

"Babe, you've got Karl eating you out and my cock in your mouth; I don't think you need to be worried about showing us your sexy little tits."

"But.....I mean........Oh fuck it," and with that, she wrapped her lips back around my cock. That was the moment that always stands out for me as the moment that Jemma surrendered to the experience, the moment her last hint of modesty disappeared.

No amount of porn could ever top this, and trust me, I had watched about 99% of all amateur cuckold and hotwife porn out there. But none of it compared to the scene in front of me. The scene where my stunning partner of three years had another man indulging in her precious pussy, while she worked her mouth around my throbbing cock. I wish I had grabbed my phone and taken a picture or a video, anything that would have captured the moment.

As Jemma continued to work her lips around my cock I knew I wasn't going to be able to last much longer.

After a few minutes, Jemma also brought her other hand down and completely surprised me by placing it squarely behind Karl's head. I looked down to see her burying her fingers in his hair, taking a good grip and pulling his head forward, burying it even deeper between her legs.

I heard a little chuckle from Karl and then a muffled comment, "That's it, girl, show your fiance what a dirty little slut you can be."

That comment seemed to flip a switch for Jemma, whether it was being called a slut, or being asked to perform and show me how dirty she could be, but something changed at that instant. She took her lips off my cock immediately but kept her eyes shut. I knew what was about to happen before it actually did. I looked down and saw Jenna's sexy legs start to shake, just a little at first, but building up until it was an uncontrollable shaking on either side of Karl's head. Then she let out an incredible moan, which can probably only really be called a scream, as she lifted her stomach and gripped the couch for dear life. If Tasha was awake, then she would definitely have heard Jemma cumming from Karl's tongue.

The sight of Jemma lying back on the couch, her stunning little body writhing around as she came harder than I'd ever seen, was the final straw for me. I took hold of my cock, which felt like steel in my hand, and stroked away the last remnants of self-control I had. A second later, my whole body shook as I exploded all over my fiancée's strained face. Her eyes were closed so she wouldn't have seen what I had just done, but my near screams of joy and the feeling of the biggest load I had ever produced landing on her face would have given away what had just happened. The feeling of cumming was unlike anything I'd ever experienced before. It was so powerful, like raw energy exploding from my cock.

Neither of us moved for what felt like an age but was probably only a few seconds. We just stayed there, breathing heavily until, eventually, she brought both hands up and started to wipe my cum off her face. Jemma was never the biggest fan of cum on her face, and I began to think the high was wearing off and she was going to be annoyed that I'd cum all over her without warning. But then Jemma opened her eyes, smiled a sexy smile at me, and said, "Someone couldn't control themself," and with that, placed her fingers in her mouth and sucked some of my cum off her fingertips.

I very nearly passed out with shock.

Instead, I collapsed beside my fiancée on the sofa, and we both started laughing, but Karl's voice soon reminded me that this was real and that he was still there.

"So, now it's my turn, right?" Karl said as he was slowly backing away from the couch. As he looked up at Jemma, we could both see his lips glistening with Jemma's pussy juices.

"Huh?" Jemma simply smiled. "I think you've had enough, don't you?" As she said it, she winked at Karl, and it amazed me that my sweet and innocent fiancée still had the sense of humor to tease him after such an intense moment.

"Oh no, Jemma, I'm far from done," Karl replied, as he quickly dropped his pants and slid his underwear off his legs.

Jemma and I both looked at each other, pretty surprised by this. I guess we had both just cum as hard as we'd ever cum in our lives, which would normally be a pretty fair indicator that sex was over.

But after we shared that look, I watched as Karl stood up. He was standing right in front of Jemma, with his cock sticking straight out in front of him. And my God, was it an impressive cock. I'm not small; in fact, I've never worried about the size of my cock. Partly because Jemma has so little to compare it to but also because I know I'm pretty solidly above average. Just over 6 inches long and a very solid 5 inches of girth (yes, I have measured and looked up the stats) meant I was bigger than most guys. But I felt seriously small compared to what Karl was pushing in front of my fiance's face right now. He must have been 2 inches longer than me, but it was the thickness that almost killed me. I know it wasn't because it's impossible, but it looked like it was twice as thick as mine.

He placed his hands on his hips as we stared at his huge cock, "See that, Rich? I can tell you're impressed?"

I was pissed at this comment. It was so rude, so unnecessary. Everyone in that room at that moment knew he had a huge cock, and knew it was bigger than mine. Why did he feel the need to say it out loud? But weirdly, I also didn't care at all. I guess this was normal after fantasy fulfillment type sex. I was full of so many good feelings; even the feeling of being pathetic and inadequate compared to the cock my finance was about to get just faded into the background.

"Fuck you, man. It's not even that big, really," I laughed a little as I said it.

Jemma looked away when I said that, unable to hide her smile. She was able to mutter, "Come on, Karl! I've already seen it. Stop showing off. It's nothing that impressive. It's just a big willy" before slowly trying to slide up from the bottom of the couch where she had been made to spread her legs, to a more natural position closer to me.

"No way," Karl cried as he swiftly bent down and grabbed Jemma's tiny wrist, pulling her body toward him. "I saw what you were doing to Rich. It was so hot. You were absolutely incredible with your mouth, and I think I deserve a little reward too!"

Jemma looked back at me with a shocked expression on her face, the exact same one I would have had on my face too. Maybe the look of shock was there because she expected me to stop him? Or did she expect me to stop her?

Chapter 7

I felt the familiar feeling of sickness rise in my stomach. Until that point, everything had been a game. The die determined what we did. It wasn't us. It was destiny, the universe, God, whatever. Now, suddenly, it was us in control. It was some dice game telling us what to do. It was Karl putting his big hard cock in Jemma's face and asking her if she wanted to suck it while I was sitting there! Even though I thought I was done with this fantasy when we both came, there was still something incredibly exciting about seeing his cock only inches from Jemma's face. I didn't know if I wanted to get off this ride just yet. But if I'm honest, I was scared to stay on.

Karl was clearly not willing to give up and call it fantasy fulfilled at that stage, and he pulled Jemma by the wrist again, moving her face so it was right in front of his hard cock. His big, hard, swollen cock was only inches from her face. She looked small and timid underneath Karl, and I could tell from his face that he loved that.

"Babe..." was all I heard her say as Jemma tried to turn away again and slide back towards me. This time Karl placed one hand on either side of her head and used them to turn it back towards him. "No way, babe. It's my turn now. You're going to show me that naughty side of yours that Rich's been hiding all for himself. You know you were fucking wet when you held my cock earlier. Rich, you know your dirty little slut of a fiance wasn't just holding my cock earlier when she had he back to you. You know she was jerking me off, right?"

Jemma thought of saying something sarcastic in response at this point, but all she could see was Karl's cock, rock hard and leaking a glob of precum, just an inch away from her face. That and what he had just said was entirely true. She had definitely done more than the game instructed her to. She felt guilty about it, but her pussy was aching. She looked at Karl's cock once more. His big, rock-hard cock, fuck, she wanted to do this. She had never been more turned on in her life than she was right then, thinking about his massive cock that she was about to taste.

Jemma blinked as she inched her lips closer to Karl's huge cock.

"Is this... I mean, is this what my fiancée wants me to do. This is what he fantasizes about, right? He told me about it. He said he wouldn't be mad if I gave another guy head. Besides, it's only going to be this one time, and he's sitting right there." That was Jemma's thought process as her mouth slowly closed around the head of Karl's massive cock.

Karl's eyes widened as he saw Jemma's mouth close around him.

Jemma paused for a second with just the head of his cock in her mouth. She couldn't actually believe what she was doing. Was this considered cheating? She knew she wouldn't cheat with anyone! But now here she was, giving some guy head while her fiance sat there and watched. She felt so incredibly slutty about herself. But she didn't feel bad about sucking his cock, not even slightly.

I couldn't see what Karl was seeing; I could just see the back of Jemma's head bobbing up and down and the side of her mouth. I could see it was wrapped around his cock, but I couldn't really see her lips or anything like that. But what I could see was more than enough to start getting me hard again. And that was utterly insane, given I'd just cum, at most 2 minutes ago. It normally took at least an hour for me to be able to get hard again, sometimes longer, so it showed just how incredibly hot the scene was. It was impossible not to get turned on watching my gorgeous fiancée's toned back and arms moving in rhythm as her head bobbed up and down, giving this asshole the best blowjob he'd ever had. I wish I had a better view, but the sight from where I was sitting was still driving me absolutely wild. I just couldn't seem to move.

"Oh, fuck Jemma. You don't mess around, do you? That's some fucking insane blowjob skills. Holy fuck! Don't stop." Karl's words and contorted facial expression were telling quite the tale.

Something I'd started to pick up on was that whenever Karl said something a bit risqué, it really seemed to get Jemma going. Like when he called her a slut!. I guess I should have known that about her! I should have known it turned her on, and I should have used it as a way to excite her. But I had never done it. I had never called her a slut. She wasn't a slut; she was my fiance. She wasn't some slutty girl, she was my fiance, and she was only sucking this massive cock in front of me to fulfill my fantasy. "

"That's it slut, suck that cock. You love a nice big cock in your mouth, don't you, you dirty little bitch?"

As Karl said the words, I could see Jemma's sucking speed increase. She was eating up the insults. She loved them, and with every insult, I could see her putting more effort into stroking and savoring Karl's enormous cock,

"Yeah, that's it slut. Look at me while you suck my cock. Oh, look at you; I bet you've never had anything that big in your mouth before, have you?'

Jemma never answered, she just kept bobbing her head up and down, but Karl clearly wanted an answer, as he took hold of her hair and pulled his cock from her mouth.

"I asked you a question slut. I said I bet you've never had anything that big in your mouth before, have you. Your fiance can't compare to this cock, can he slut?"

Jemma turned her head to look at me. I could see the fear in her eyes. She didn't know what to say. Was she really about to say, out loud, to her fiance that she was sucking a bigger cock? We both knew it, but saying it out loud was a different matter. Then Jemma smiled. At first, I couldn't work out what she was smiling about. Then I realized. I was still sitting there with no pants on, and as I looked down, my cock was rock hard. Jemma had clearly seen my erection and smiled. With that, she looked back at Karl and looked up at him.

"No, I've never sucked a cock like this before, and no, there's no way he's ever going to be able to compare to this. Your cock is fucking huge."

Then Jemma paused and quickly looked back at me once more before looking back up at Karl.

"God, I wish he had a cock like yours. I'd give him so much more head if he did," and with that, her mouth closed around Karl's massive cock again. What she had just said hit me like a freight train. It hurt a lot. I knew he was bigger, but saying it like that was just savage. She didn't have to say she wished I had a cock like his. And what a total bitch saying I'd get more head if I had a cock like him. I couldn't believe what had just come out of my fiance's mouth. What a little slut.

As I thought about what she said repeatedly, I couldn't help but start stroking my own again. I was so hard, and the sounds Jemma was making were sounds I didn't hear when she was sucking my cock: it was like she was sucking on a lollipop that was way too big for her mouth.

"Rich, dude, where have you been hiding this filthy little slut?" As Karl said that, he reached behind Jemma's head with both hands, encouraging her to pick up the pace.

As she looked up at him, he smiled down at her and said. "That's it, slut. Look right at me. Get your slutty mouth ready!"

I noticed Jemma pick up the pace even more as he said it. Her muscles were tensing all over her body now, and the fact the living room was only lit by the lamp accentuated her glistening, fit body as she continued to pleasure another man in front of me. If she had been some chubby little slut it would be understandable, but for some reason, her muscular, toned body made her look powerful and dominant. Like she should be saying no to him unless, of course, she wanted to suck his cock. Unless, of course, she was doing this for herself and not for me!

"I fucking love your cock. God, it's so big. I'd suck this for you every day if you were my boyfriend."

At that moment, I thought back to when she last sucked my cock before tonight. It was three weeks ago. And that was too much. Despite my earlier cum explosion, I let out another huge jet of cum that landed on the floor between me and my fiancée.

She didn't even notice.

Karl didn't notice me cumming either. He was too deeply immersed in what was going on right in front of his eyes. Jemma continued to bob up and down with real passionate movements that made me a little jealous. I genuinely couldn't remember her ever sucking my cock that passionately. I saw when Karl could no longer resist, and he just shut his eyes, and his whole body tensed up while he held Jemma's head over his hard cock. I could actually hear her choke a little as Karl emptied his balls into her throat. I could also see where her hands were. She had them on his legs, and she made no movement at all to push Karl away. In fact, as I looked again, it looked like she was gripping him tightly. I would find myself reliving this moment again and again for days afterward. Jemma was never a huge fan of cum swallowing, and I had never seen her grip my legs and almost force me to cum in her mouth. But she did that for Karl.

After what seemed like an eternity, Karl released his grip on Jemma's head. And he staggered backward, almost crashing into the television behind him. I could see he left a sweaty palm print on the screen.

"Holy fuck, Rich... she really is a keeper!" His breathing was almost out of control as he placed his hands on his head. "And she swallows!"

I focused my slightly blurred vision back onto Jemma, who began to slowly turn around to face me. I would never have described Jemma as a swallower before.

As she turned to face me, I could see what a mess her face and hair were, and I could see the trails of my cum were still on the side of her face and down her body.

Until the day I die, I will never forget the look she gave me at that point, accompanied by a sly smirk, as she licked her lips and asked, "So, was that fun for you, baby?"

I just sat on the sofa, completely stunned.

At this point, almost like it was timed to perfection, we heard flushing coming from upstairs. With that, Karl jumped up, wasting no time at all, grabbed his clothes, and put them all back on.

"Okay, guys, listen, that was a lot of fun, but I gotta go!" He looked a little worried, but at the same time, he looked happier than I'd ever seen him.

"Oh, and thanks, Jemma. You really are one hot little slut!" He whispered as he disappeared up the stairs and into the night.

Jemma was now just lying on the couch. Her legs were dangling off to the side as she just stared up at the ceiling. Then she sat up straight and looked right at me.

"Well, you didn't answer me."

I sat there motionless for a few seconds, trying to compose my thoughts, before crawling over and hovering above her face.

"That was fucking amazing, babe. You were so sexy. Holy fuck, it was out of this world."

Jemma frowned as I said it, which I really didn't expect. I thought I'd just paid her a compliment.

"Babe, I did that for you. I don't even like Karl!"

I continued to hover over her, my blank expression perfectly mirroring my confused feelings. I took a moment to think about what she was saying before I slid my right hand up and between her legs, right up until my fingers were pressed against her pussy. It was wetter than it had ever been.

"That was really... all just for my benefit?" I asked, with an incredulous look on my face.

As soon as I said it and gently ran my hand along her pussy, Jemma went bright red almost instantly, her playful green eyes staring deeply into mine. Then her serious look broke, and out came the smile.

"Well. Maybe not entirely for you." She said as she brought her hands up and cupped my face, planting a sloppy wet kiss on my lips, "I might have enjoyed it just a little bit."

I kissed back, and soon our kiss on the lips had turned into a deep passionate kiss with tongues. I was fully aware of where Jemma's mouth had been, I could smell it on her, and as our tongues danced together,

I could definitely taste it on her. But I didn't care. My sweet innocent fiancée had just turned into my personal porn star right in front of my eyes. She had just given me the best show I would ever see in my entire life. As we sat on the sofa making out, my hands continued to feel her body, and a few minutes later, I started to finger her. I couldn't resist asking her another question. It was one I needed her to answer right away. I pulled back from the kiss momentarily and looked her in the eye.

"What now?"

I was expecting a shy answer; I was expecting Jemma to be coming down from the high of that night's events and to suggest something tame at best. Her answer truly shocked me and set the tone for the rest of our relationship.

"I think it's time you tried to reclaim your fiance, don't you, babe? You can fuck me and see if you can stop me from thinking about his big hard cock while you do it." As she said that, I felt her hand on my cock, impossibly hard again.

"Do you think your little cock is up to the task, baby?"

The rest of the night was pretty tame compared to what had happened so far; it was just me and Jemma. I definitely made her cum a few times, but as we lay in bed afterward, I asked the question.

"So babe, whose cock were you thinking about when we were fucking."

"Yours babe, 100%," was the reply, the best reply I've ever heard.

"I was definitely thinking about yours and how much better it would feel if you had a cock like Karl." With that, she kissed me on the lips and rolled over. A few minutes later, Jemma was fast asleep, snoring away, and I was sat up in bed, devastated. I couldn't believe what she said. I felt so humiliated. I sat in bed awake for hours, humiliated and embarrassed, with the biggest hard-on I've ever had.

I knew at that moment I didn't want to be a cuckold, but I definitely was!

Don't miss out!

Visit the website below and you can sign up to receive emails whenever Leigh Temple publishes a new book. There's no charge and no obligation.

https://books2read.com/r/B-A-FTIR-YPDKC

BOOKS 2 READ

Connecting independent readers to independent writers.

Also by Leigh Temple

First Time Hotwife In Cancun
Housewife to Hotwife
Becoming a Hotwife - A Wife Transforms Before Her Cuckold
Husband's Eyes
Anniversary Swinging: A Couple Look For New Ways To Celebrate
The Cuckold Clinic
Vacation Cuckold
A White Wife Can't Resist
First Time Entered
Cuckold Cleanup
Control
Hotwife Surprise
A Shared Submission
Pushing The Boundaries